Open the Casket
J. N. Eagles

Open the Casket

Copyright © 2023 by J. N. Eagles

All rights reserved. No part of this book may be reproduced, stored in a retrieval system, or transmitted in any form or by any means—electronic, mechanical, photocopy, recording, or any other—except for brief quotations in printed reviews, without the prior written permission of the author.

This is a work of fiction. All characters are fictitious. People, events, incidents, descriptions, dialogue, and opinions expressed in this work are products of the author's imagination and are not to be construed as real.

First Edition 2023
ISBN: 9798373275569

Cover designer: Jeanette Barroso
Illustrator: Elise Pullen

Other Works
by J. N. Eagles

Kings and Queens
Beneath the Ocean
A Beach for Us

To my family and friends,
I'll love y'all even those on the other side.

Contents

An Unmarked Grave……………………………………..9

Woman in Mourning……..…………..…………….39

Haunted…………….…………………………….…115

Part I
An Unmarked Grave

Open the Casket

A skeleton, so clean
that upon first inspection no one
could distinguish who it belonged to.
Bones without a name.
Remains left untouched.
A body concealed
beneath their feet.

Every grave possessed a marker
except one without a stone displayed.
Each mourner was unaware
that a lost soul roamed near.
Not one noticed me,
though I kept vigil over the buried.

Open the Casket

Not too young, not too old,
just enough ticking to question everything.
When my time finally came,
I closed my eyes
and said hello to death.

J. N. Eagles

Gateways sealed,
Raining dirt on top.
Abandoned my body,
Voicelessly screaming
Even though my heart stopped beating.

Dirt and grime encapsulated my body. I broke free from my physical form, yet remained trapped. Without hands, I dug myself out of the darkness that laid heavy around me. Once I escaped, released from the dirt's clutches, I ascended until I was yanked back to the ground, free to roam the cemetery or to sleep beneath it. I glanced around at all the stones sprouting from the grass, and on all sides, a black fence surrounded me and these memorials. The gates yawned open, so I made my way toward them. As I grew closer, a vibration made the entrance swing shut. The sensation kept happening until I took a step back. Nothing else seemed phased by the tremors, even the naked tree stood still. Again, I took a step forward, and again, the vibrations started. This time they released the bolt and the gates locked with an echoing bang. This was my new home, and I wasn't allowed to leave.

J. N. Eagles

The oak tree that once grew
its bright leaves in spring
has since looked more like a skeleton.
The first greenery fell on the unmarked grave,
and since then, each casket had stripped
another leaf.
Everything near me perished.

Open the Casket

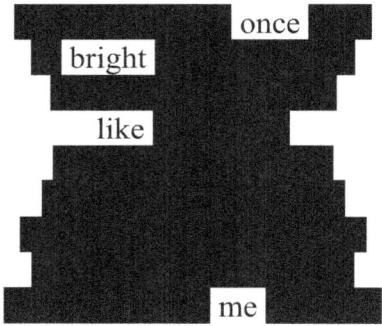

once
bright
like
me

J. N. Eagles

Tall in the middle of the graveyard,
Reaching out with arms, beckoning
Everyone closer to its wooden body.
Etched into its bark, names of the dead.

Open the Casket

Only alive to eventually die.
I didn't remember my last moments
just like I didn't remember my first.
A red apple molds and sinks into the dirt
without enough time to taste the juices of life.
Honestly, I could have stopped it,
but my existence was already wasted.

Gasping for breath I couldn't feel;
healing wouldn't happen here.
Observing my body from the outside,
something still connected me.
Truth stayed hidden when there was no reflection.

Open the Casket

Only red to taste

J. N. Eagles

Damp and cold,
Eternity spent
Alone in silence.
Timid—even wind
Hesitated to visit.

Open the Casket

They were not here,
yet I was.
Their silence mocked
my struggle to vanish.
It was their clear engravings
that I must turn away from,
but I couldn't.
I couldn't stand as still as them.
So, I wandered and memorized their inscriptions:
A good husband, a wonderful father.

Once, we were both alive,
breathing at the same time,
but now we were both deceased.
Bones without flesh,
branches without leaves.
I felt my roots deep,
entangled with the tree.
If the tree was ever cut down, gone,
would I be too?

Open the Casket

The gravedigger only visited
when there was a job to do.
As the holes were filled and covered
with dirt and grass and flowers,
each of them were labeled with a stone.
Everywhere I looked, I saw their identities,
and I found myself hating their names
because, from left to right, they all had something,
except for one.

J. N. Eagles

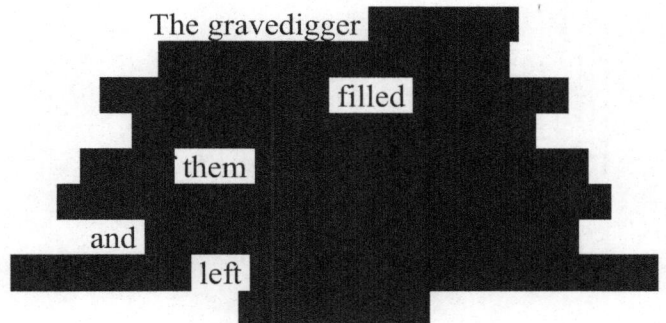

The gravedigger filled them and left

Open the Casket

On special occasions,
the gravedigger had a duty
to place a bouquet on every grave.
Never once did he lay one on mine.
Flowers never survived more than a day.

J. N. Eagles

The gravedigger skipped laying bouquets
on the grave below his feet.
He wasn't to blame
for the unknown dead,
though I tried to show him
by laying stolen flowers on top.

Open the Casket

The digger surveyed two graves
as no other site would be proper.
He readied himself to dig a small hole,
but there wasn't enough room
between both stones.

J. N. Eagles

If the tree was removed,
there'd be more room
in the overcrowded cemetery.
The large oak wouldn't be missed,
because it was already dead.

Open the Casket

Though dead,
its deep roots still
held the tree upright.

When the day came to chop the tree, I flinched as the last, withered leaf drifted to the ground. The ax bit into the bark repeatedly. It was like someone being slashed at the whipping post, the wounds turned to scars on their back. Though a ghost, I tried to take a stand. I stood in front of the trunk and each swing of the blade sliced through my neck. Deceased as I was, it didn't bother me, but still, I yearned to save the dead tree.

The falling timber crashed
to the ground and splintered.
So thunderous of an impact,
I was surprised none
of the dead stirred.

J. N. Eagles

Temporarily, a short stump
marked its place.
There, the digger sat to rest
with his back turned to the fallen branches.
Perhaps he refused to face what he had done,
but I stared at the dead tree
in the blinding sun.

Open the Casket

Finally, the digger stood
and grabbed his shovel.
He started prying
the stump from the ground.
The hole grew perfectly
wide and deep.
When the trunk came out,
it was a good size,
for the hole wasn't too large,
but smaller than I thought it would be.
The digger wasted no time
and laid the dead to rest in their casket.

J. N. Eagles

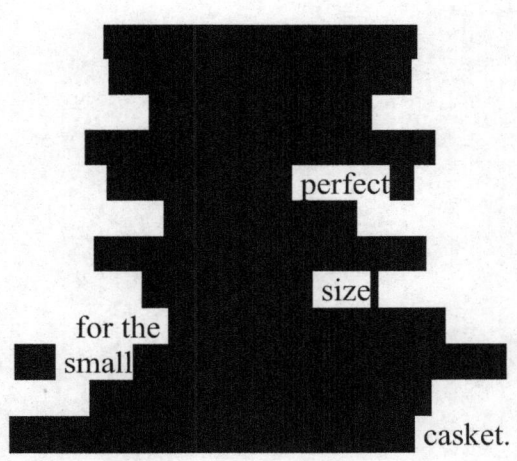

perfect

size

for the
small

casket.

The living didn't acknowledge
the missing tree, nor did they notice
the new stone in the graveyard.
No, they'd rather keep their heads down
and ignore that they'll eventually
end up here, too.

J. N. Eagles

I kept waiting for it to happen,
but it never did.
Though I searched the burial ground,
I never saw the child's ghost appear.
I wondered why.

Open the Casket

It had to be the tree.
He chopped it down,
and now there was no shade
in the entire cemetery to rest beneath.

Part II
Woman in Mourning

Open the Casket

Muddy boots in a drizzle.
Opened umbrella, set aside.
Unused since it didn't stop the cold.
Remorse.
Numb.
It was what I imagined,
Never going through grief myself.
Gates closed on me before anyone I loved died.

She came to pay her respects
with blooming red carnations.
Could have been for her wedding day,
yet the color was pale.
For every breath inhaled,
she released a shaky exhale.
Gently placing the bouquet she held dear,
she whispered, *If only you were still here.*

Though lonesome she stood
in front of that stone,
I wish I could tell her that
within this silent gravesite,
she didn't stand alone.

In time, the flowers
she placed on the ground
eventually perished.
Dried petals
cast from their stems
scattered across the cemetery
until one found its way to me.

If I could have touched it
as gentle as moonlight,
I would have,
but even that would not
be tender enough.
The wilted petal
diminished to dust
as quickly as it had come.

J. N. Eagles

She visited so often
it was as if she lived here.
Cheeks wet, she'd fall asleep
at the grave, headstone her pillow,
soft moss her bed.
Sometimes, I wondered
if she dreaded waking up.

Open the Casket

I wanted to console her,
to stroke her cheek,
to show her I was near.
Finally, I found the nerve
to stand before her,
but she looked right through me.

J. N. Eagles

Perhaps, one day, she'll decide to move on.
All my hopes for us to unite, long gone.
Though there'd be a hole in my time,
a purpose remained to watch over the grave.
If what happened to me,
happened to her—dead to ghost—
then I would be there to lead her to the tree.
Except it was gone, no longer a guidepost.
Eventually, there will be a place here to lay,
but nothing to convince her to stay.

Open the Casket

For so long the tombstones stood
that their bases grew weary
and their forms leaned.
Blankets of soft moss
covered their bodies,
engravings faded from tired faces,
slowly degraded.

I could visit every gravesite,
run an invisible hand across each rock,
and tell them how sorry
I was they were gone.

But the dead couldn't talk to me,
nor could the living.

Open the Casket

If tombstones could talk,
they'd tell me how they
grieved that I stayed.

Thieves entered through the gates
and laughed nervously,
visiting my haunted cemetery
with hopes of stollen riches,
completely oblivious to the spirit
that dwelled here.
They searched for a stone
without mourners.
They searched for the empty
grave full of rumors.
They searched with lanterns
bobbing in the night.
Light beckons me to follow.

Open the Casket

They visited the burial ground
almost every night, sneaking jewelry
from silent caskets, off still innocents.

Though the black gates
were locked at night,
the thieves still came.
They climbed the fence.
Despite their cunning ways,
I sympathized and wanted
to somehow warn them
that it was sometimes easier to enter
than it would ever be to leave.

Open the Casket

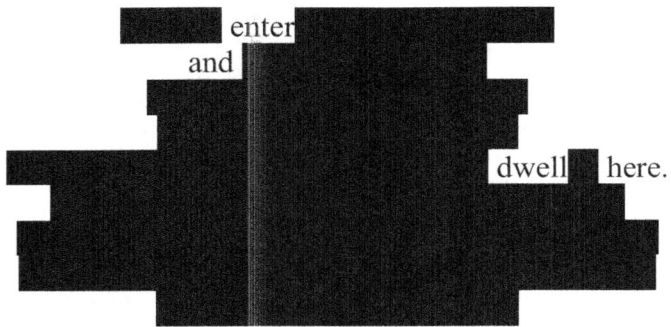

Showed up in the dead of night, uninvited,
Hunted through the graveyard,
Obtained buried treasure. The two thieves
Ventured eight feet deep to reclaim
Earthy watches, rings, and necklaces,
Luck growing with each mound of dirt.

Once they scavenged
everything they could,
they laid the dead back to rest.
A rumpled dirt blanket
thrown back on top.

Relentless, these robbers were.
They never missed a night,
and no one ever noticed
the riches disappearing.
In the morning, the gravedigger
straightened the flowers
and moved on to the next.

Open the Casket

Each time
the gravedigger tidied the bouquet
the woman left,
I caused them to bend over again.
Whether it was a stiff breeze
or a warm breath, it didn't matter.
With twisted stems, they would remain.

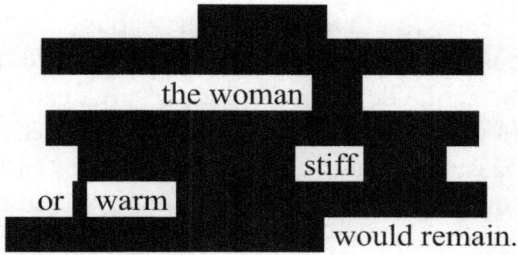

the woman
stiff
or warm
would remain.

Open the Casket

They found more than they sought.
A ghost who preferred company over solitude.
Standing in the dew, on the edge of my dead grass,
I waited patiently for the thieves to inch closer.
Like passing through a door, they stepped inside.
Goosebumps rose on their arms. They cowered in fear.
Finally, they realized I was near.

J. N. Eagles

Once, they dug up an old coffin.
The graverobbers pried it open
and uncovered a beautiful corpse.
She was buried in a lavish white dress,
which they stole from her sleeping frame,
leaving the bride
in her casket
in the rain.

Open the Casket

The broken casket was surrounded
by markers all bearing the same name.
There was no one left
to venture deep into the graveyard
to notice the casket and the bride
covered with mud.

J. N. Eagles

These thieves took their time,
in a place people wished they had a little more.
They scoured the burial ground,
searching for their next dig.
They spotted one with a bouquet
that seemed rather fresh,
perhaps because it was different from the rest.
Shovel to dirt, they crept lower
until I had to lean in
to see their bodies working
the casket open.

One kept peering over his shoulder
and wondered aloud,
I feel like someone is watching us.
The other laughed and shook his head,
but they both dug a little faster.

The thieves worked
quieter than the dead.
The burial ground had never
been so silent.
I wondered
if they could hear me.

I think they felt my presence.
Small hairs stood on end
off the backs of their necks.

I think they saw my shadow.
Their faces turned pale, eyes wide.

I think they heard me whisper,
warning them to *stop*,
but they ignored it.

I couldn't let them
steal anything
the woman cared for.
I'd rather die.
I knew I should stop them,
but why hadn't I?

Open the Casket

Who was it she mourned so much?
If I knew, I'd understand her better.
Perhaps I could talk to her,
tell her it's okay to grieve.
She can visit as often as she'd like;
she'd never have to leave.

Oh, but what a private thing
it was to grieve.
To hear mourners weep,
invading and making me ill.
For even in my ghostly form,
I sometimes felt a chill.

Open the Casket

Temptation too grand,
I floated nearby
and eagerly waited
as they opened the coffin.

Closed off from the rest of the world,
A body laid untouched inside.
Surrounded by soft silk,
Kept as pristine as it was visitation day
Elbows bent, hands on chest.
Tomorrow would be the same.

Open the Casket

After so long underground, it surprised me
to see his body perfectly preserved.
Wondering how that was, I crept closer
and peeked at the crisp clothes,
reached as if to touch
his cheek and wake him from slumber.
An odor announced its presence.
Though time slipped by,
the stench of alcohol remained.

J. N. Eagles

So, the man was a devoted drunk.
I could see it clearly, drinking
until his liver resigned,
seeping his life away.
The part I didn't understand
was why the woman cared for him.
He had the kind of face
that could easily be forgotten.
If it was up to me, the man would be.

Open the Casket

What the woman
found was most precious
in her mourning,
was most precious to me.

The thieves worked
the deceased's ring off his finger.
I could not let that happen.

With a force I couldn't explain, I possessed the closest robber. His mind, sticky with thoughts reeking as bad as decay, fought for a moment, and then renounced control to me. I moved his arms easier than I had moved mine when I was alive. I made him shove his partner into the grave. Making sure he was comfortable next to the dead man, I sealed the cover. As he lay beating and screaming, I used the thief to shovel dirt on top. It took the rest of the night, and with sunlight stretching through the cemetery, I released my control and watched the other robber hesitate, and then he ran for the gate.

J. N. Eagles

Cozy holes in the earth,
Easy to fall asleep in.
Mounds of blanketed dirt,
Evidence hidden. It leaves
The gravedigger suspicious,
Ear close to the ground.
Resting they were supposed to be,
Yet screams came from deep inside.

The graves weren't safe
as long as the last thief still visited.
He hadn't gotten away.
I could feel his warm body near,
but didn't know where.
I searched for him,
gliding through the tombstones.

Too bad the silence of the burial ground
made his breathing louder.
I found him near the gates.
Almost, he escaped.

Open the Casket

Rocky terrain
Offered hiding places.
Behind a stone, he cowered,
But the living couldn't dwell.
Eerily he breathed and clutched the ring
Radiating in the dark, dark night.

J. N. Eagles

I came to him,
and the air
froze.
So cold,
he couldn't remain
still.

Open the Casket

He shivered and shivered
until I believed
even his corpse would tremble.

J. N. Eagles

With lantern held high,
the robber saw my shadow
hanging over him like the grim reaper.
I offered my hand to him.
As a wetness seeped through his pants,
he placed the ring on my palm.

Using all my strength,
I kept that jewel
close to my chest
and couldn't stop him
from running out the gate.

Open the Casket

How simple for the living
to leave and not return.
I waited long nights for the thief to appear,
either to steal again or to visit the rock
which his partner lay beneath,
but I never once saw him again,
not in old age and not in death.

J. N. Eagles

As for the one who was buried alive,
oxygen slowly dwindled in his confinement.
However grotesque it was to share
a coffin with another dead,
and a few minutes left to spare,
the doomed robber seemed
to have accepted his fate.

Silently, he waited in the casket,
exiled and betrayed by his own.
He killed time by counting ghosts.
Little did he know that I watched
through the eyes of the corpse
everything in those final moments.
Over and over before running out of air,
he etched a message into the wood using his nails.

The vision I borrowed was blurry,
like tears filling, but refusing to fall.
Eyes heavy with sleep,
refusing to stay open,
as I tried to read the inscription.

Though it was darker inside the coffin
than it was in the corpse's mind,
I could pick out pieces
of what the robber wrote.
Stole for you.
Whoever *you* was,
they must have been worth the risk.

J. N. Eagles

Leaving this body,
guilt followed me above ground
for it was the man
the woman had mourned.
I eased into his dead mind
easily, and besides it being stiff,
the body was willing.
Though I shouldn't have used him,
I knew I had to.
No matter what,
I wouldn't let someone
suffer death alone.

Open the Casket

I guarded the grave,
not wanting the digger
to discover two in one hole.
Though he seemed wary,
he left it as it was.
Now that the thieves
stopped visiting,
the digger roamed
the burial ground more often.

J. N. Eagles

I saw him more often than the woman,
and since I knew I could possess,
I tried to take charge of him and walk out the gates,
but his body evaded me.
His silhouette slipped between my fingers
like wisps of fog,
refusing to grant control.
I could rule over corpses, and manipulate thieves,
but I couldn't, no matter what,
enter the mind of the gravedigger's.

Open the Casket

The woman was older now
with thin, graying hair
and wrinkles around her eyes.
She entered the cemetery slowly,
didn't linger too long,
and walked gradually back toward the gates.

It felt like I was chained
to my resting place,
stuck on the ground or beneath it,
and even if I broke free,
the cemetery gates remained locked.
Not allowed to follow her out
to the land of the living.

Open the Casket

I've been there for her,
helped tidy the tombstone,
protected it from thieves,
and listened to her cry,
yet she never noticed me,
too distracted by her mourning.
I've always been jealous of the dead,
but this one surpassed all the others combined.

I took a moment to glance
around the burial grounds.
Every grave had a marker except one.
It needed a stone,
though there were none to spare,
something to stop the living
from walking past
without a glance.

Open the Casket

The unmarked grave was the first.
All the others dug around it
as if it were the center of the cemetery,
and the tree, older than any of the dead,
should have been there to shield it.

J. N. Eagles

When I saw the woman,
closing in on the gate,
I steeled myself
and inched forward,
sneaking, trying not to startle her.

Despite how often the digger cared for the dead, the tree had never received the same treatment. Its bones still lay in the middle of the cemetery, decomposing slowly, its arms rigid and brittle. A ghost I was; I took the woman like I had taken the robber. Without consent—I was sure I'd remain here for eternity—I forced her to do my bidding. She moved as I commanded and dragged the dead tree to the spot where the unmarked grave sat for centuries. We spent hours digging through the ground with her bare hands. Dirt collected beneath her nails. We uncovered the body and rearranged its position. With my ghostly capabilities, the woman managed to sit the tree up right. The body embraced it as we continued to pour soil over them until the skeleton was covered and the tree seemed as if it stood alone. After a short rest—I didn't want to strain her poor body—we went to work carving the tree. When we finished, a new inscription told each passerby, dead or alive, that a man had fallen asleep here.

J. N. Eagles

Several feet below the ground's surface,
Kneeling with the trunk in his arms, but
Everything else in the graveyard waited.
Layers of death and decay settled as
Everyone seemed to hold their breath,
Though most didn't have breath to hold.
Omen or not, a gust twisted among the branches.
Neither the tree nor the corpse stirred.

Open the Casket

Worse than thieves,
I hated that I had to steal her body.
Her mind was like a willow
dancing in a breeze.
She let me in,
and in the same manner,
she let me leave.
It was nice enough,
but I felt guilty.
She stumbled when I left her thoughts,
like she was stronger with me there,
unsure what to do without me.

It was inevitable that the woman would die.
When her body finally came to rest,
would she be buried here, next to the grave?
More than that, would she feel called to stay?
Part of me wished she would,
but another part never wanted
to see her again.

If we never met again,
it would mean that she truly moved on.
Wouldn't that be better
than being trapped here?
Though I would die
for another chance to see her,
how could I confess
that I've watched her for years?
Ashamed I had taken her body.

All this tension weakened her heart.
Too much strain and it finally ruptured.
I saw it happen.
She stood and turned away from the tree.
When she reached the gate's black bars,
she glanced over her shoulder,
in the direction of the marker,
but her eyes seemed to settle on me.

I swore when she spoke, she spoke to me
in a voice that could warm a cold body.
*I can't do it anymore. I'm sorry,
but I'm not coming back.*
Her lips quivered with each word
and her hand reached for the gate,
knuckles turning white
as soon as they touched the bars.

J. N. Eagles

She collapsed.
I knew she died
as soon as her body hit the ground.
It was as if the cemetery
refused to let her leave.
Finally, it seemed the gates
worked on my behalf.
I desperately wanted to
see her again.

Open the Casket

I waited with her and watched
her body lose its warmth
until the gravedigger found her.
He took her away, so she could be prepared,
face powdered and fresh clothes donned
for her return confined in a coffin.
But when he started to dig her grave,
next to the one she visited, I felt reconnected.

J. N. Eagles

I remained there when they placed her
into the ground and tucked soil neatly on top.
I was there when her tombstone was set
above her head like a crown and even after
grass grew back over the dirt mound,
but still she had not returned,
and my hope of reuniting slowly withered.

Open the Casket

I had watched her mourn for years.
Now that she was gone,
who was there to mourn her?
No one ever accompanied her, except me.

J. N. Eagles

I always made
sure there were
flowers on both
their graves.

Whether or not I ever saw her again,
I'd still guard these two headstones
for as long as I remained.

J. N. Eagles

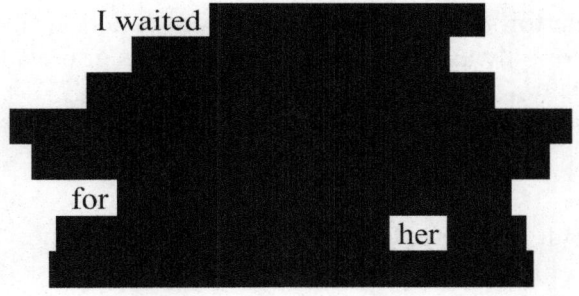

Open the Casket

Gone for years and without another called to stay,
would it always be me who haunted this graveyard?
Was it the oak's roots that trapped me?
I had hoped that restoring the tree
with the skeleton would undo
whatever curse there was.
But still here, I stood above the small stone,
the one that had replaced the tree,
and not for the first time,
I wished the child had lived.

I've had a lot of lonely nights
here among the buried,
but this one—her anniversary—was darker
and there seemed to be no break of dawn.
Always, I had watched her,
though she hardly ever looked my way.
I waited near her grave, patient for her return.
Although she never promised to stay,
I'd keep waiting even if she didn't.

Part III
Haunted

Open the Casket

I needed to return what the robber took,
but I couldn't dig up the casket.
Instead, I set the ring in front of his stone.
So close to hers that I couldn't stop myself.
I read
and read
and read
the engravings:
A good wife, a wonderful mother.

J. N. Eagles

In time, she found me.

Open the Casket

She returned with the morning fog.
It cloaked her, embracing her body.
I couldn't see where she stood, could only hear
her voice calling out as if she were the ghost.
The fog was so thick that my cemetery
was shrouded in white
like a bride's veil on her wedding night.

J. N. Eagles

Open the Casket

She returned as my bride

J. N. Eagles

The morning's white haze
evaporated in the sunlight.
Even though the air was empty,
I searched for her—her spirit, her soul,
her ghost.

Open the Casket

Briefly, I wondered
if she had turned back,
trying to leave
through the black gates.
Perhaps she hadn't realized
she's without her body.
A blank reflection in a puddle.
How lost she'd be,
when for the first time,
the door refused her.

Casting deep shadows,
the gate loomed before me.
Subtle vibrations started as they did before,
warning me to not draw any closer.
Its iron bars strong and ancient,
but without rust, stood
ominous in the short distance.
Though fingers of sunshine
reached inside the cemetery,
they embraced nothing.
No one lingered near the gate.

I searched for her in the clear morning.
I went to the grave she always visited,
studied the inscription and flowers
and noted the cold, hard ground.
The ring hadn't moved from where I set it.
Of course, she wouldn't return here.
She'd finally moved on from her mourning.

I found her underneath the ghost of the tree.
She clung to the dead trunk, embracing it
as if the branches would catch her
if she started to drift up.

Despite how many years had passed,
it was all in accordance with her soul and spirit
that she looked the same as she did the first day.
Her ghostly form returned her to a younger age.
Her appearance made me want to peer into a mirror.
Though no reflection would stare back,
I wanted to know if I looked as young as she.

I drew closer to her,
asking her not to fear.
Nothing to force her to depart.
I knew this because I had tried
and never managed to float away.

Open the Casket

I   fear.

to float away.

J. N. Eagles

She wondered how it was possible
that we were still here
after our bodies had expired.
The truth was I didn't know.

Once, I would have guessed that the tree
only called to certain people
and sometimes they listened,
but since the tree was removed,
I didn't have a clue.

Open the Casket

When the thieves dug up the grave,
beneath the tomb she had mourned
was a body I easily recognized.
Through much consumption,
the alcohol preserved him.
Even after all these years,
one thing was clear in the moonshine:
the still crisped tuxedo was mine.

J. N. Eagles

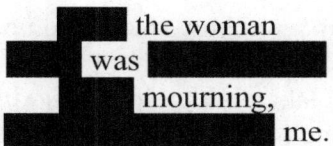

Open the Casket

She wondered how she ended up here.
So, I told her what I knew.
I had taken her to do my bidding.
The force of me possessing her collapsed her body,
and the gravedigger, as his duty, buried her next to me.
That was his duty—to take care of those
who could no longer sustain
what raged inside.

The gravedigger,
he kept the cemetery,
kept the graves,
kept the flowers,
but she never noticed him.
Not when he stood
in the same spot each morning
as if he knew what lay beneath his feet.
Different from her, I saw him clearly,
and different from her, I couldn't possess him.
He was like me.
The black gates kept him.

Open the Casket

I gestured toward the unmarked grave,
where a new tree stood to indicate it,
but he was not there.
Already, the digger was straightening flowers
left in front of headstones.
Shifting slightly, I noticed a little light
shining through his silhouette.

J. N. Eagles

The unmarked grave
never once had so many
acknowledge it.
Yet, the gravedigger
still eluded us
for his skeleton held the tree
and his wandering soul
seemed at peace,
silently waiting for an end
that wouldn't come.

Open the Casket

Did the digger chop down the tree
solely so he could place
a small stone next to two,
or did he kill the tree
because it could have been that
which summoned us to stay?

If he cared for all the dead,
then why did he skip me?
He never once cleaned my marker,
the words slowly fading under moss.
Nor did he ever place a bouquet.
He didn't help me move on,
not when I arrived,
and not when she died.

How had I not seen it?
This hole between us
was all of me.
When dirt covered me,
I was born a ghost.
My past life was lost.
I wondered why
she mourned me so long.

I had to ask her why, why did she grieve for me so long? Finally, when the truth settled within me, deep like roots, I understood. I remembered that when I drank, I wasn't angry. She was thankful for that. I didn't have much to offer her after I had lost my job, our house, and all our savings. She should have left me a long time ago, but she didn't. Of all the decisions I made, choosing her was the best. She said she'd choose me over and over again. Though I had failed her in many ways, I was always there for her. I gave her my shoulder, I gave her my time, I gave her space and a listening ear. After I passed away, I was there for her in my ghostly form.

Open the Casket

J. N. Eagles

She needed me in other ways.
After I had passed,
I couldn't wipe her tears off her cheek.
She couldn't hear my voice one last time.
We couldn't hold each other's hand.
She didn't know I stayed near;
all she knew was that I wasn't there.

Open the Casket

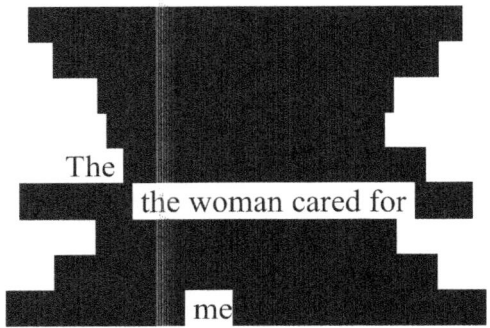

J. N. Eagles

I refused to look away, fearing
that when I looked back, she'd be gone.
She, however, dropped her gaze,
claimed I needed to move on.
Her whisper filled the cemetery
like a bird's song.
I'm glad you moved the tree.
Please, don't feel guilty.

Open the Casket

Her ghost sparkled in the dawn.
She wasn't going to wait until night.
Raising her open arms,
it started with her fingertips.
They vanished,
then her hands,
and shoulders.
Her silhouette glowed
as if she was the sun
until I had to turn away,
and when I looked back,
she was gone.

Laying together, apart
In caskets only.
Vital it was for me
Impossible to ascend
Needed her to first be
Gowned in light.

My hand, mere inches from her.
Again, I was refused her touch.
She appeared next to the tree,
and her ghost vanished just as quickly.
The moment was not enough.
At the same time, it was too much.

Breathing in the morning air,
I closed my eyes and opened my arms,
just as she had done,
ready to receive, ready to leave.

Open the Casket

I waited. I waited
and waited
and waited
and waited.
When I opened my eyes,
the graveyard surrounded me still.

J. N. Eagles

I stopped just before the trunk
and breathed in deep, stale air.
Contrasting the stench of decay,
a sweet aroma engulfed me.
Past where the woman's silhouette had stood,
the tree's bones once stiff and empty
were dotted with tiny green buds
and embraced in child laughter.

Open the Casket

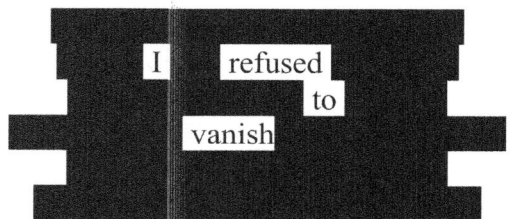

J. N. Eagles

The souls returned once the tree
was secure in its final resting place.
I knew if I let it, the wind that rustled
between its branches would take me away,
but what if the digger took an ax
to the tree again and demolished it?
The child that died so long ago
and buried between their parents,
wouldn't be able to leave.

Open the Casket

I yearned to follow my wife; too many years apart,
but I still couldn't depart from the cemetery,
partly my guilt and partly
because other lost souls would be called to the tree.
I couldn't leave them.
The digger preserved the graveyard,
but I tended to the tree and to the ones who stayed.

J. N. Eagles

Rest wouldn't come to me.
In the day and in the night,
Peace continued to wave goodbye.

The following is an extract from *Beneath the Ocean*. Available on Amazon as a paperback, hardback, and an eBook.

Part I
A Splash

Everything within me
kept shutting down.
In the undertow
of myself,
I felt like I was drowning.

Everything around me
kept closing in.
In the undertow
of it all,
I felt like I was drowning.

Not until a mirror was found
tangled within my fishing net
did we understand riches existed
in the middle of the ocean.
Gems decorated the glass.
The golden handle weighed down
my hand, but the sailors took it,
carrying it away and concealing it from me.
They set our course for the island,
not realizing how delicate
a reflection could be.

That mirror, I had gazed upon its glass,
saw my face for a fleeting moment.
I didn't recognize my appearance,
smudges of dirt, sunburnt skin,
tired eyes, and thin unsmiling lips.
Could this mirror be the first of many treasures
which would bring our sailing to a halt?
Claiming the riches could end our eternal search,
finally, able to rejoice in our farewell to the ocean.

The island, about which we only heard whispers.
The riches there could deliver us home,
but that place was so far away. Not sure of the direction.
Not sure if I wanted to return there.
Only sure of the direction of the treasure island—out to sea.
The sailors would rather be lost and searching,
than simply lost like me.

Once, we thought we saw
a silhouette on the horizon,
a long, lowly shadow that resembled
our vision of the treasure island.
Though we sailed toward it,
the waves kept us at bay.
Constantly, the sailors stared into the mirror,
but, just like the horizon,
they never saw what they desired.
Then one foggy morning, the island
disappeared, and still we sailed
not knowing if we'd glimpse the outline again.

It seemed like a lifetime
that the sailors and I searched for the island.
Supposedly, when we landed there,
we were to find a chest hidden
beneath a warm blanket of sand.
Buried just below the surface,
treasure waited for us to claim it.
It seemed like a lifetime
that we sailed across the oceans,
day and night and day and night and day and night,
but we never came closer to the island or its promises.

Deep was the ocean, but my mind went deeper
Eerie were the trenches of my thoughts
Paradise didn't exist for me
Realized the island might never be in sight
End end end end end end—will it end?
Swallowed the ocean until not a drop was left
Swore to myself I wouldn't survive
I did.
Ocean proved me wrong, stayed a little longer
Never gave in to the monsters inside

Tossing my net onto the wooden deck,
I climbed the railing.
Wind whipped my hair,
tugging as if beckoning me to step off.
I turned to check if the crew watched.
But while one was busy at the wheel,
and the other tightening the sails,
the waves continued their reach for me,
quietly whispering that they'll catch me.

I took a breath,
a deep, deep breath.
Not knowing if I would get another chance,
but knowing that this was a better chance
to find the island rather than sailing,
I closed my eyes and
jumped.

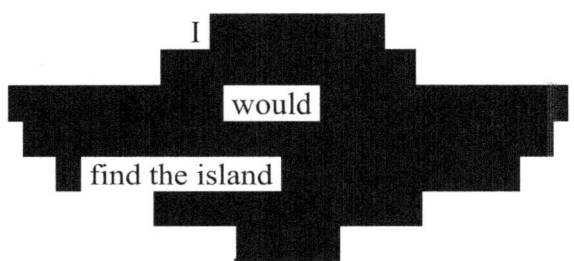

I would find the island

Shocking, icy water embraced me
Pivotal moment as my senses awakened
Like it was the first time that I've
Actually felt, and felt more in these few
Seconds than I had on the boat in years
How was I supposed to deal with this?

Acknowledgments

Thank you to my husband, especially for the time you spend with our daughter. I love seeing you two together and miss y'all when I go to write, even if just for an hour. You're always my first reader and always patient with me, though I may sometimes be impatient for you to finish reading my stories. Thanks for reading this one quicker.

Thank you to my father for your constant support. It means the world to me that you believe in me and in my writing. I'll make you proud.

Thank you to Jeanette and Elise, my team. Y'all's artwork is the first thing readers see, and I wouldn't have it any other way. Also, a big thank you to my beta readers and editors, especially Brooke and Tarah. This story, as with all my others, needed some polishing before it was published.

Thank you, readers. Thank you for taking the time to read my poems, writing a review, and for even trying poetry if this isn't your typical genre. I hope I didn't scare you away and that you keep reading poetry even if it isn't mine. There are a lot of great poets out there. I hope you find one that becomes your favorite and you get the chance to read all their books.

About the Author

J. N. Eagles currently lives in Alabama with her husband, daughter, two cats, and a flock of chickens. She runs a reading blog where she posts reviews about the books on her shelves, and she plans to write many books of poetry. She graduated from Athens State University with a Bachelor's in English/Language Arts and graduated from the University of North Alabama with a Master of Arts in Writing. When she's not reading or scribbling new stories, she enjoys the outdoors and working in her garden.

Website: jneaglesbooks.com

Instagram: @j.n.eagles.author

Facebook: @J. N. Eagles

Printed in Great Britain
by Amazon